THE KING'S QUEST

A DRAGON LORDS OF VALDIER SHORT STORY

S.E. SMITH

MONTANA
PUBLISHING

ACKNOWLEDGMENTS

I would like to thank my husband Steve for believing in me and being proud enough of me to give me the courage to follow my dream. I would also like to give a special thank you to my sister and best friend, Linda, who not only encouraged me to write, but who also read the manuscript. Also to my other friends who believe in me: Julie, Jackie, Christel, Sally, Jolanda, Lisa, Laurelle, Debbie, and Narelle. The girls that keep me going!

And a special thanks to Paul Heitsch, David Brenin, Samantha Cook, Suzanne Elise Freeman, and PJ Ochlan—the awesome voices behind my audiobooks!

—S.E. Smith

The King's Quest
A Dragon Lords of Valdier Short Story
Copyright © 2021 by Susan E. Smith
First E-Book Publication March 2021

Summary: A quest to save his world leads a King to a Goddess.

ISBN: 9781952021879 (paperback)
ISBN: 9781952021862 (eBook)

Romance (love, suggestive sexual content) | Fantasy | Science Fiction (Aliens) | Royal | Contemporary | Paranormal | Novella | Action/Adventure

Published by Montana Publishing, LLC
& SE Smith of Florida Inc. www.sesmithfl.com

CONTENTS

SYNOPSIS

King Tamblin, ruler of the Kingdom of Glitter, prepares for battle after the aliens foretold by his sister, Tia, return to his world. He will stop at nothing to prevent the creatures from decimating their small moon again. Yet, there is little he or the Kingdom of the Sand People can do to stop the invasion. With all hope fading, Tia tells him that he must go on a quest to find the beautiful and mysterious Arosa, Queen of the Wood Fairies, and ask for her help.

Arosa, considered a Goddess on many worlds she visits, is stunned when a playful trick to entertain the Dragonlings of Valdier turns her life upside down. She never expects to feel the strange yet exhilarating emotions that Tamblin stirs inside her. Her kind were supposed to observe other species, not fall in love with them!

When the small bat she sent to guard over Tamblin alerts her that he is in danger, she will risk breaking the rules to protect him. Arosa recognizes love, but will the King return her feelings when he discovers that she is more than just the Queen of the Wood Fairies—that she has the power to not only save his world, but create entire galaxies?

PROLOGUE

Kingdom of Glitter:

Minor Moon of Leviathan

Several Months Before the Present

"Oh, Arilla, what have we done?"

Arosa mentally sent the silent, dismayed question to her sister, Arilla, a moment before she solidified into the form of the Queen of the Wood Fairies. She caught the little girl who had slipped from the balcony high above and tightly cradled her. Hope, the daughter of the twin dragons, Cree and Calo, and their human mate, Melina, tearfully clung to her. She could feel Hope's heart pounding with fear. Mortified by the near tragedy, Arosa tenderly rocked the girl as she whispered soothing reassurances that she was safe.

Arosa landed outside of the palace where Hope had slipped from the balcony just seconds before. An instant later, Cree and Calo's symbiots touched down beside her. Their golden bodies were pressing against her to reassure themselves that their tiny charge was safe.

Arosa tried to smile reassuringly at the two almost identical dragons that swooped down, shifting into men a split second before they landed. The heart-wrenching fear on both men's faces tore through her, causing a rush of emotion that manifested into a physical pain inside her chest.

"Hope," Cree choked out, his arms reaching for his tiny sobbing daughter. "Daddy's here, my little dragonling."

"We're here. I'm so sorry, my little princess. We should never have left you," Calo said in a thick, trembling voice. "Goddess, how can we ever thank you for saving our daughter?"

Arosa stared at the two men. "I'm not…," she began before a child's excited voice pierced the air.

"It's the Queen of the Wood Fairies!" Morah Reykill happily exclaimed.

Arosa silently groaned when she saw the group of younglings gathering around her. Caught, she wasn't sure what she should do. When—not if—Aikaterina found out about this, Arosa suspected Arilla and she would be chastised.

She looked down when a tiny hand slipped into hers. Morah Reykill gave her a huge grin and an exaggerated wink, then stared at her with shining eyes full of excitement.

"I's knew you was reals," Morah cheerfully announced.

For a moment, Arosa struggled to remember who she was supposed to be. She frantically reached out to Arilla as she tried to decide the best way to handle the situation. Arilla's soft, lilting laughter filled her head when Tia, the Keeper of the Stories for the Kingdom of Glitter and their secret accomplice in this misadventure, stepped forward with a warm smile. Beside her was a stately man that inspired an unexpected response inside her.

Tia smiled and waved her hand between the man and Arosa. "King Tamblin, may I introduce the Queen of the Wood Fairies…," she began before she paused.

Arosa realized that Tia was waiting for her to introduce herself. "Arosa…. My name is Arosa," she replied, clasping her hands in front of her and folding her wings.

"Arosa," Tia repeated with a gentle smile. "Arosa, may I introduce Tamblin, King of the Leprechauns of Glitter."

Arilla! What am I to do? Arosa silently groaned to her sister.

Be the Queen of the Wood Fairies, sister, Arilla faintly replied.

An hour later, Tamblin smiled and distractedly nodded when one of the men sitting around the fire said something he didn't quite catch. Whatever it was must have been funny given the deep male laughter surrounding him. Tamblin was fascinated by the group of children as they joyfully played under the watchful eyes of their fathers.

He decided that tonight could only be described with one word—magical. It was hard to believe the strangers sitting around the fire were Valdier, Sarafin, and Curizan warriors. He remembered them being so much larger. It wasn't only the men sitting and chatting or the unusual children who shifted from one form to another who held his fascination, though. The beautiful enchantress sitting beside him was twisting his normal, stolid control into knots.

"Is everything alright?" Arosa asked.

Tamblin nodded. In an impulsive move, he reached down and cupped Arosa's hand. She stiffened with surprise and tilted her head, giving him a curious, shy look. He rose to his feet and looked down at her.

"Would you like to go for a walk?" he asked.

"I—yes, that would be nice," she answered.

Tamblin didn't miss the note of uncertainty in Arosa's voice. Paul Grove, one of the men sitting around the fire, looked up and gave him a nod. Tamblin bowed his head and smiled before guiding Arosa away from the group and along a cobblestone path. The stones lit up under his feet but not hers. It took him a moment to realize it was because she was floating beside him, not actually touching the cobblestones.

"Do you mind if I ask where your kingdom is? I have never heard of it before," he politely inquired.

Arosa gave him a startled glance and then quickly looked away. "It is in—the woods," she answered in a hesitant voice.

"Where though? The forests are just now growing back. How did you survive after the Tasiers were taken?" he asked, mentioning the small, furry rodents hunted almost to extinction by off-world traders.

"Not far. There is a forest that survived—to the west. That way," she said, with a wave of her hand, "on the other side of this mountain."

"That is north," he replied.

Arosa scowled at him. "Well, it is to the north," she said, floating a few steps ahead of him.

Tamblin tightened his grip on her hand and twirled her around. Arosa gasped when their bodies collided. He slowly lifted her hand to his lips and kissed her fingers.

"Tia has never mentioned Wood Fairies before," he said.

"King Tamblin," Arosa began.

"Please, call me Tamblin. As I said, Tia has never mentioned the Wood Fairies, but... I also have never asked about them," he continued.

Arosa nodded. "Then, that is why you haven't heard of me," she breathlessly replied.

"Queen Arosa, it would be an honor to show you my Kingdom, if you would permit me," he said, with a slight bow.

Arosa nodded again. Tamblin took a deep breath, released her hand, and held out his arm for her. She gave him an uncertain look before she threaded her arm through his.

A satisfied smiled curved his lips when she tightened her grasp on his arm. They continued along the path as it curved through a small mushroom forest to a gazebo by the river. When he needed a quiet place to sit and think, he often came here.

"How did you find your way to Glitter?" he inquired.

Arosa frowned. "I followed the men. They were looking for the King of the Leprechauns," she replied.

Tamblin's lips twitched at her tone. She sounded almost pleased with herself. He couldn't discern if she was telling him the truth or not. From the way she glanced at him, he suspected she was—but with a touch of exaggeration.

He chuckled and guided her up the steps into the gazebo. She released his arm and walked over to a small deck built over the water. He studied her face as she stared down at the colorful fish.

"Paul explained a little of what happened to them. It is a very interesting story." He paused when he heard the faint sound of music. "Would you like to dance?" he asked.

Arosa turned and faced him. Her wide eyes were filled with uncertainty. He walked over to her and held out his hand when she didn't reject his request. She hesitantly lifted her hand and placed her palm against his as he drew her other hand to his shoulder. He pulled her closer to him as they danced.

The magic of the night filled him with a sense of freedom he hadn't felt in years. Their steps were slow at first as she tried to follow his movements. He led, guiding her in the simple steps. They twirled, moving in a graceful circle. All around them, the bioluminescent spores rose into the air like floating candles while fish splashed in the water, trying to gobble up those that drifted too close to the surface.

The colors of the night danced across her lovely face, and Arosa appeared to glow. Her eyes shone with her joy, and her radiant beauty took his breath away.

He drew them to a stop when the music faded. His heart pounded in his chest as he released her hand and wrapped his arms around her waist. She looked at him with wide eyes and parted lips.

"I hope you don't think I'm too forward for what I'm about to do," he said in a low voice.

"What are you about to do?" she breathlessly asked.

Tamblin smiled and lowered his head. "This," he replied, capturing her parted lips with his.

Arosa stood frozen, unsure of what was happening or what to do when Tamblin kissed her. Well, she understood in theory what Tamblin was doing. She knew that to reproduce, species needed to interact physically.

She and her sister, Arilla, had lived among the dragons of Valdier and visited enough worlds to understand that the species developed affections for each other. In fact, she felt genuine affection for the dragonlings, the group of young children from the planet Valdier, and their friends from the worlds of Sarafin and Curizan. It was one reason she and Arilla enjoyed spending time with the children and their families, especially during their holiday celebrations.

It wasn't like they spent a lot of physical time with them. She and Arilla enjoyed observing the interactions between the adults and their offspring. There might have also been some curiosity about the physical relationship between the adults. It was impossible to be oblivious to that. She viewed it as research, for gaining a deeper understanding for the time when she and Arilla were permitted to create and seed their own worlds with life.

The twin sisters were still young compared to Aikaterina, Aminta, Xyrie, and the other remaining elders—not that there were many of them left. As Aikaterina's protégées, they were being tutored on how to observe the evolution of worlds.

Their species had been created at the same time as the universe. As the universe expanded, so had their travels. The

Elders, the first of her kind, had learned how to harness the energy that had created them. She and Arilla first appeared on the outer fringes of the universe, when it was still young and expanding at an exponential rate.

Aikaterina had discovered them drifting, their life force fading into the icy darkness of space. She had given each of them part of her own essence. It was much the same way that the Valdier could support their symbiots—the living-gold creatures that the Elders nurtured.

Arosa leaned forward when Tamblin pulled back. She liked the feel of his lips against hers. There was an energy in their shared kiss that created a spark inside her. The breath from his soft chuckle brushed against her cheek.

"That was very… pleasant," she announced.

Tamblin laughed. "Yes, it was indeed very pleasant," he teased.

Arilla silently floated above her sister and the young King of Glitter. Arosa was positively glowing. The worry for her sister ebbed. Out of the two of them, Arosa was the most fragile. She suspected that Arosa's greater need for infusions of energy was why Aikaterina was so insistent that they should remain close to Valdier and the river of symbiots.

Aikaterina had already forbidden them from interfering again after their last attempt at *helping* had ended with them accidentally sending a human ahead in time. It had been impossible to remain just an observer when the young woman's selfless courage had saved her world. Aikaterina had warned them at the time, that when timelines crossed and were altered, it created different outcomes—with consequences sometimes not seen for centuries.

Arilla sighed as a sense of guilt washed through her. She wondered if being around the Valdier, Sarafin, Curizan, and their human mates was the reason she and Arosa were more inclined to push the boundaries of what they should and shouldn't do. Arilla bit her lip and decided she needed to check on their mentor.

She looked down again when Arosa's laughter swirled through the air. Her sister would be alright. Arosa could handle the situation here while she went back to check on Aikaterina.

After all, what could happen? The Dragonlings and younglings were reunited with their fathers and would soon be home. Arosa would then return to the hive, and the King —well, he would never know that the beautiful, gentle Queen of the Wood Fairies was actually a being far more powerful than any other creature he would ever meet.

Tonight will be a pleasant memory for both of them, Arilla thought with a pleased smile before she vanished, leaving her sister to enjoy her time as a fairy tale Queen.

CHAPTER ONE

Kingdom of Glitter:

A Month Before the Present

"Tamblin, are you alright?" Tia asked, stepping out onto the palace balcony.

Tamblin nodded and glanced at his sister before returning his attention to the glittering kingdom in front of him. He wrapped his arm around her waist when she leaned against him. They stood in silence for several minutes, each lost in their own thoughts.

"It's beautiful. I think the festival this year is the best we've ever had," he said.

"They've always been wonderful, but I have to agree. I love this time of year when the mushrooms release their spores. You must come visit the Sand Kingdom again soon. The dunes are lit up at night. It reminds me of this place." She sighed with contentment. "Jett's mother and father are debating on whether they should change the name of their kingdom now that the desert is shrinking. The mushroom forests are spreading at a phenomenal rate. It reminds me of the old illustrations," she replied.

"It won't be for long if what you told me this afternoon comes to pass," he grimly replied.

Tia squeezed his arm. "My vision—maybe it won't come true," she wistfully countered.

He faced her. "Your visions have never been wrong, Tia. You know that. When the aliens return to our world, we must be ready this time. I want you to remember that there is plenty of room for expansion here. I will write a missive to Jett's parents, letting them know that the people of the Sand Kingdom are welcome here," he said.

Tia shook her head. "You know that would never work, Tamblin. Jett and his people will never give up their home without a fight," she replied.

He sighed. "If the aliens come, they may not have a choice. We are no match for their size and strength," he said.

Tia parted her lips as if she would protest, but she closed them and nodded instead. He pulled her into his arms and hugged her tight. Her slender figure had filled out again, and it felt good to hold her without fear of breaking her.

"How have you been feeling?" he asked.

She laughed and shook her head. "You ask me that every time you see me. I'm fine, Tamblin. My heart is beating normally. If it wasn't for running after my little Arielle, I would be the size of a Tasier with the way I eat," she retorted, referring to the furry rodents crucial to their small moon.

Tamblin chuckled and released her. "I think you are perfect." He turned and looked down over the kingdom again. "I can't believe how fast Arielle is growing. Though, I think she takes after your husband more than you," he said.

Tia put her hands on her hips, raised an eyebrow, and gave him a pouty look. "Why do you say that? I think she has a lot of my qualities," she replied.

He waved a hand over the railing. "You haven't been watching them, have you?" he asked with a laugh.

Tia followed the direction he was pointing. She uttered a very unladylike curse under her breath, hiked up her skirt, and left at a run. Tamblin laughed and shook his head. He gripped the railing and watched with amusement as Tia burst out of the palace below and hurried down the steps. His brother-in-law, Jett, was going to be in big trouble this time—not that he wasn't in it most of the time.

Jett appeared to have decided it was time to teach his petite daughter how to sword fight—albeit with a diminutive wooden sword. From the way Jett was yelping, hopping around, and rubbing at his shins, Tamblin was sure the man was already regretting the decision to give his little Arielle this lesson.

His niece also appeared to have inherited a bit of her personality from the woman she was named after. It had surprised him when Tia and Jett named their daughter after the alien female—but it was also fitting. Tia had foretold that a woman from a distant world would bring life back to the barren moon they called home. Once again, his sister had been right.

Lady Ariel of Valdier had discovered the Tasiers—gentle, furry beasts that ate the sandworms and fertilized their planet—at an off-world market. Unbeknownst to her, the creatures were essential to the ecological survival of the small moon and its inhabitants. The few she had brought with her had reproduced quickly—especially on a diet of sandworms. A chemical reaction between the spores buried deep in the sand and the excrement from the Tasiers caused forests of giant mushrooms to grow. The mushrooms rose from the vast deserts, cooling their world and bringing the much-needed cleaner air and rain.

Tamblin chuckled when he watched Jett laughingly trying to evade the dual attack of Tia and little Arielle. The sounds of boots against the polished stone floor pulled him away from his view of the activities below. He frowned when he saw the brooding expression on his General's face.

"What is it?" he demanded.

General Brant and two of his men halted at attention. Brant bowed his head in greeting before meeting his gaze. "King Tamblin, it is as you warned us this morning. We have spotted alien ships to the north," Brant responded.

Tamblin clenched his fist. "How many?" he demanded in a hard voice.

"Two, your Grace," Brant answered.

Two—so far. This would be just the beginning if history were to repeat itself. While Mandra Reykill, a Dragon Prince of Valdier, had declared the moon a sanctuary, the price for Tasiers was too tempting for some traders to resist. The dragon-shifters had long considered the small rodents a delicacy.

Now that the mushroom forest was thriving, the gentle creatures flourished. The moon was finally healing from the predation. Now it was being threatened again.

Tamblin gave a brief nod. "I want you to gather an elite reconnaissance team. See if you can board the ships without being detected. We need to know how the ships operate and discover if there is a way to disable them," he instructed.

Brant frowned. "If we disable the ships, it will trap the aliens on the moon," he warned.

Tamblin gave him a grim smile. "Yes. It is vital we have a strategy that will level out the battlefield. We are no match for their technology or their size. We will need to use what we have to our advantage. For now, we should assess the situation and gather as much information as we can," he replied.

"I'll gather a team, and we'll leave this evening," Brant said with a bow. Turning on his heel, he left.

Tamblin looked out across his kingdom again. The sounds of music and laughter resonated throughout the cavern. Illuminated mushrooms growing in thick clusters with brilliant colors released spores that looked like floating candles. Soft breezes that blew through the open vents would help carry most of the seeds outside where they would mix with the other spores.

The mood of his people had changed over the past few years. The restored balance of the moon brought feelings of joy and hope, while the discovery of other clans outside of the cavern brought a chance of survival. Tia's union with Jett had paved the way for increased trade and introduced the possibilities for new relationships among the clans.

He briefly closed his eyes when a shaft of yearning pierced him. The memory of Arosa, Queen of the Wood Fairies, flashed through his mind. He had not seen her since the night the men and children of Valdier had visited. His responsibilities always seemed to impede his own desires.

There hadn't been a day since then that he hadn't thought about Arosa. He would remember that magical night with her for the rest of his life. Memories burned inside him: the way her four small transparent wings hung down her back like a cloak, the way her long hair, its vibrant color like flames capped by a crown of tiny white flowers with dark red berries, fell over her shoulder, and the rosy hue of her lips after he kissed her. He would never forget how her brilliant green gown fell in layers around her, a striking contrast against her red hair and silky skin. Her intellect and wit had truly captured his admiration.

"Tamblin."

He turned when he heard Jett call his name. Lost in thought, he had missed the sound of Jett's approach. He forced a smile of greeting on his lips.

"Jett. I see you escaped your wife and daughter relatively unscathed. It looks like you might have a bruise under your eye by tomorrow," he mused.

Jett touched the tender spot under his left eye. "Arielle caught me with her sword while doing a backhand twirl. She said she is a dancing warrior princess," he chuckled before growing somber. "Santil found me. He said the scouts had spotted two alien transports."

"Yes. I've sent a team to do reconnaissance," he said.

Jett nodded. "I've done the same," he replied, walking over to the railing.

"I was going to send a missive to your parents. I want you to know that the Sand People are welcome here," he said.

"I appreciate the offer and will convey your message to my parents," Jett replied.

Tamblin didn't miss the way Jett's hands tightened on the railing, nor the way his lips pursed. They stood in silence, looking out over the festivities. He was about to say something when Jett spoke.

"Perhaps they will leave. The Dragon Lords promised to protect our moon. Surely whoever the traders are would not dare cross such powerful creatures," Jett growled with frustration.

"Greed can be more powerful than the need to survive, Jett. Generations ago, our ancestors saw what it could do. Almost three-quarters of our people died because of hunger, loss of habitat, or through the aliens' careless harvesting of the Tasiers. Only a few clans survived the devastation by the aliens, and we didn't even know about each other until recently," Tamblin reminded him.

"We can't let it happen again, Tamblin," Jett passionately declared.

"It won't. We will fight them," he replied, his eyes glued on Tia and little Arielle's laughing faces.

"Is there any way to get in touch with the Valdier?" Jett asked.

"They will know. The question is if they will discover it in time," he reluctantly admitted.

Jett frowned and faced him. "What do you mean?" he asked.

Tamblin sighed. "The Valdier promised to protect our planet. The last time Lord Mandra returned, he asked me if I would agree to the Valdier sending a scientific research ship here to install devices that would monitor the rehabilitation of the moon. I agreed, and now once every new moon, the information automatically transmits to them through these devices," he said.

"My parents mentioned it to me when you relayed the message to them, but where did they install them? I haven't seen any of the devices," he replied with a frown.

"There are four within a hundred-mile radius. One in each direction. I was told that if there is a dramatic change in the readings, it will trigger an alert, and someone from Valdier will come," Tamblin explained.

"It will be another thirty days before the moon circles the planet. Our historical scripts state that it took less than half that time for the population of the Tasiers to drop to critical," Jett growled with frustration.

"There were more ships," Tamblin pointed out.

Jett shook his head. "There were a lot more Tasiers, too," he countered.

Tamblin nodded. "Let us hope that these two ships are the only ones and we can discourage them from staying," he said.

"How do you propose to do that?" Jett muttered.

Tamblin sighed. "By any means necessary. We'll start with the Guardians," he said.

Jett shuddered. "Are you sure? Those beasts are as dangerous as the aliens," he muttered.

"That is what I am hoping," Tamblin grimly replied.

CHAPTER TWO

Minor Moon of Leviathan:

Present

Tamblin stared out at the lights flickering across the vast mushroom-covered plains. His heart ached when he heard the frightened squeaks of the Tasiers and the sharp snap of a trap. Despair filled him when he saw the poachers trying to reach the traps before his or Jett's men could.

The last weeks had grown decidedly more perilous. The two transports had become four, then six, and eight. He had ordered General Brant and his elite squad to disable the transports, but the aliens repaired them almost as quickly as they sabotaged them. It had finally become too dangerous. The poachers had set traps, injuring two of his warriors. Another six men had been trapped inside a transport that was about to leave the planet and they had barely made it out.

Tamblin released a sigh when a furry head nudged him. Oversized brown eyes with gold flecks in them gazed back at him with a solemn, inquisitive expression. He lifted his hand and gently scratched the adolescent bat behind one of its oversized ears.

"It's alright, Batty. Let's hope Jett and his teams get to the traps before the poachers," he tiredly said.

Exhaustion fogged his mind. This was the third week that he, Jett, and a combined force of soldiers from Sandora and Glitter were out all night. The poachers had begun patrolling when they realized that their traps were being sabotaged.

Batty nudged him again and turned his ears in the direction of the bouncing lights. Tamblin nodded his head in acknowledgement. Batty wanted to fly, and Tamblin needed something to lift his spirits.

"Your mistress would be very proud of you," he affectionately said.

Batty wiggled his ears back and forth, making Tamblin laugh. He stroked the bat for another moment before he turned and climbed onto the saddle strapped between its wings. He reached up and adjusted the night vision goggles over his eyes. With his focus on the vast plains below, he gripped the reins and tapped his heels to Batty's side.

"Let's have a little fun," he said.

Batty twitched his ears back and forth with delight, then jumped off the edge. Tamblin leaned forward and tightened his thighs against the saddle as they soared downward until finally, Batty began flapping his wings.

The wind brushed against his face as they flew through the night. It was going to be another long one. From the air, he followed Jett's team as they moved quickly to release the Tasiers that had unwittingly entered the traps.

"To the left, Batty," Tamblin instructed, leaning in the saddle.

The bat darted in front of one massive poacher. The man stumbled back several steps and swiped an enormous hand in their direction. Batty twisted in midair, changing directions. The man tried to follow their movements, twisting around so fast that he lost his balance.

"Damn creatures," the man growled with frustration.

Tamblin gritted his teeth when the man pulled a laser pistol from his waist and aimed the weapon at them. He leaned forward and Batty swerved. Tamblin winced when the super-heated blast from the laser narrowly missed them.

"*Dragon's balls, Macron!* Are you trying to kill me?" another poacher yelled when the blast sent him diving for cover.

"Sorry, Harron. These bats are driving me crazy," Macron shouted back, quickly holstering his weapon.

"You shoot that thing again and it will be more than the bats you'll have to worry about. The trap is empty again. I swear when I find out who is releasing the furballs, I'm going to roast them," Harron said.

"This one is empty too. I hope the others are having better luck than we are," Macron replied, kneeling next to the trap.

Tamblin saw Jett and Santil crouching behind a large mushroom only a few feet from Macron, which was too close for comfort. They couldn't keep this up. It was only a matter of time before someone was killed.

The sound of another trap springing and the squeal of a Tasier pulled him away. Batty flew in that direction, trying to reach the poor creature before the two poachers. Tamblin tensed, preparing to jump.

This will be another close encounter, he grimly thought as he released his grip on the reins and fell toward the large mushroom that would soften his fall.

Valdier:

The Hive

Arosa lay along the bank of the river of symbiots and moodily swirled a finger in the flow of gold. Warmth flowed upward through her outstretched arm. She sighed when some of the gold formed into fish and jumped. The scene reminded her of the magical night several months ago.

An uncharacteristic feeling of frustration flashed through her, and she sat up. She growled when the symbiots formed an image of Tamblin. They were reacting to her thoughts— and her longings that were growing stronger every day.

"This should not be happening," she snapped.

The symbiot gold Tamblin melted back into the river. Arosa stood up. She was alone at the moment—thankfully. With a sigh of resignation, she reached out to her sister.

Arilla, I need your guidance, she confessed.

Silence greeted her, the same silence that had surrounded her since her return from Glitter. She floated over to a boulder. Time normally meant very little to her species, but the last few months had seemed endless.

Her mind had replayed the magical night over and over. She felt guilty for her desire to go back in time to relive it, but a smile played on her lips as she closed her eyes and floated higher in the air. The wind became music in her ears.

She lifted her arms and twirled, dancing the way she had with Tamblin. She had repeated the movements so many times, she could now gracefully dance. A wave of symbiots rose from the river and formed Tamblin again. They had been her dance partner, but even their warmth could not replicate the feeling of being in his arms.

As the music faded, she opened her eyes. She traced the curve of her symbiot partner's cheek. The gold shimmered under her fingertips as it recognized her loneliness and longing.

"What is wrong with me?" she asked in a confused voice. "There is a beating in my chest that I don't understand, and I yearn for his touch. What is it that causes me to want to be with him? To hear his voice, his laughter, and to touch his lips with mine?"

She touched her mouth as she remembered his kiss. The symbiot Tamblin shifted into a bat. She shook her head and scowled at it.

"I know," she grudgingly said, turning away.

It would be so easy to spy on Tamblin. In fact, she had done so the first few days after that night, but guilt and other unfamiliar emotions plagued her, so she had forced herself to stop. At least she knew he was safe.

She floated over to a pillar and studied the star chart engraved on it, locating Tamblin's small moon. She looked at the platform and then down at the main gateway. Aikaterina and her sister still had not returned. There was no telling when they would. If she opened the main gateway, others of her kind would immediately sense it.

She looked at the pillar again. If she opened a very narrow gateway to the past, she could relive the night one last time. Perhaps the night was not as wonderful as she remembered.

"Just once, then I will never relive it again," she whispered.

The symbols on the pillar glowed as she sent the mental command. A hologram of the glowing star chart appeared before her. She touched the galaxy, pulling the moon into view. With a twirl of her fingers, time reversed until she saw the images of dragonlings. She replayed the night, following the events as they unfolded.

Her heart ached when she saw Hope's excitement turn to terror, the moment Morah gripped her hand so that she couldn't escape, and when Tamblin cupped her hand and helped her to her feet.

She stared up at the platform. The time when she was standing in Tamblin's arms appeared on the platform. She floated until she was level with the ghostly vision of her past.

"Just this one time," she promised herself and floated forward, merging her present self with her past.

A soft gasp slipped from her. Tamblin caught the sound when he kissed her. Arosa melted in his arms, wishing she could keep this moment frozen for eternity.

The Kingdom of Glitter:

Several Months Ago

. . .

"That was very... pleasant," she announced.

Tamblin laughed. "Yes, it was indeed very pleasant," he teased.

Arosa leaned forward and parted her lips when Tamblin kissed her again. She wrapped her arms around his neck and threaded her fingers through his hair. She could sense his surprise—and feel his growing desire. She sighed in regret when he reluctantly pulled back and gazed down at her.

"Arosa—I...."

She laid her fingers against his lips. "I want you to know that tonight is a night I will never forget, Tamblin," she confessed.

He frowned, slightly shook his head, and captured her hand in his. "You say that as if we will never see each other again," he said.

"My... kingdom differs from yours," she replied, pulling out of his arms.

He tightened his grip on her hand. "Things are different now. With the Tasiers' return, the mushroom forests are thriving again, and the threats have been mitigated. There is no reason we can't continue to see each other," he protested.

A pang of guilt pierced Arosa. How did she explain to Tamblin that she was not who she was pretending to be? As far as she knew, there had never been one of her kind who fell in love or stayed with another species. It was not their way.

She pulled away from him, fluttering her hand to her chest as she realized what she had just thought. Shock and confusion swept through her. Was it possible that she—a being made of pure energy—could experience love?

"Arosa, perhaps I've overstepped my boundaries, but I have to confess that I've never felt this way about anyone before. I want to see where it leads. A union between our two kingdoms could only strengthen them," he said,

"A union—?" she repeated, looking up at him in shock.

Tamblin groaned and shook his head. He reached out and cupped both of her hands in his. It was impossible for her to look away.

"That was very forward of me… but, please, hear me out. I know that we've just met, but I believe that there is a connection between us too powerful to ignore. This is an extraordinary night and I… I would like to explore where it could take us. What I'm trying to say is… I want to get to know you," he declared.

"Tonight…," she began, pausing and reaching out to her sister in desperation as she tried to think of what to say.

"We'll start with tonight," he agreed with a tender smile, misunderstanding her hesitation.

She nodded. Even though Arosa knew what was going to happen, she embraced the evening. Reliving the night over again was as magical as it had been the first time—though it seemed shorter.

All too soon, they were returning to the palace. She kissed each dragonling's forehead when they came up to wish her a goodnight. An unexpected burning stung her eyes when Morah tugged on her skirt. She knelt, looking the little girl in the eyes.

Morah touched her cheek with tiny fingers. "I wants you to knows that if you ever needs help, I will helps you. I'm goings to be a Priestess one days," she said.

Arosa smiled. "You will be a very good Priestess to the symbiots, Morah," she replied.

Morah nodded. "I's knows a lots 'causes I'm smart likes my mommy and daddy." Morah threw her little arms around Arosa's neck. The goddess blinked in surprise. "Thanks you for making my wishes come true. For my last wishes, I'd like for all the daddies and us to be bigs again so we can goes back home to our mommies."

"When you wake, your wish will have come true," Arosa promised.

"I hopes your wishes comes true too," Morah whispered in her ear before giving her a kiss on her cheek and stepping back.

Arosa stood and watched as the little girl, her skin dyed green from playing in the fountain and princess gown stained with dirt from adventuring through the land, ran over to her father. Deep in her heart, Arosa knew it was time for her to leave, but she didn't want to. She stared wistfully at Tamblin. He was talking to Paul, but she could feel his focus on her.

Anguish filled her as she relived the last few hours that she would ever have with Tamblin. A part of her wanted to pull away so she wouldn't have to say goodbye to him again, but another part wanted to savor the beautiful memory that came next.

"I've had a room prepared for you," he said.

She nodded, gripping his hand. They walked in silence up the steps into the palace. She followed him up the stairs to a long corridor on the third level. He slowed as they neared a set of double doors.

"I hope you will be comfortable. My room is next door should you need anything," he said as he turned and faced her.

"What if I need you… to stay with me tonight?" she quietly asked.

CHAPTER THREE

Minor Moon of Leviathan:

Present Day

"Tamblin, call them back," Jett shouted.

Tamblin lifted the curved horn to his lips and blew. The Guardians skidded to a stop. They were boar-like creatures with long tusks, sharp quills, and red eyes that could see in pitch darkness. One beast snarled when a blast from a poacher's laser pistol grazed it.

They couldn't afford to lose any more of the creatures that protected them. The poachers had already killed five of the beasts. Tamblin pulled back on his reins, directing Batty to follow the retreating warriors.

They were losing the war. Hundreds of Tasiers were being loaded onto the ships by the hour. Tamblin and his allies could no longer keep up with the traps. The poachers had modified the locking mechanisms, making the cages virtually impossible for his and Jett's forces to open them and free the trapped Tasiers.

They also had a bigger issue. One alien now knew about their existence and the man was hunting them. It was only a matter of time before the other poachers believed him.

Batty flew to a tall outcropping of rocks a short distance away. Nature and the weather had sculpted the various layers of rocks until it looked like slabs had been stacked on top of each other. Batty turned and gripped a large slab by his feet under a low overhang of rock.

Tamblin released his grip on the saddle, and slid off, landing on the ledge below. He lifted the horn to his lips again. He gave two long and one short blast. The Guardians responded by melting away into the night, disappearing down camouflaged holes that would lead them back to their caves.

He lowered the horn to his side when Jett's skimmer swung around an outcropping of rocks and came to a stop nearby. Jett dismounted and climbed toward his position. Tamblin reached down, gripped Jett's hand, and pulled him onto the ledge. Jett shook his head and gazed out at the trampled fields of mushrooms.

"They outnumber us, Tamblin. Even with our combined forces, we are no match for the aliens," Jett said.

"You're bleeding," he replied.

Jett grimaced and touched the wound on his temple. Tamblin walked over to Batty and pulled out a small first aid kit from his saddlebag. He motioned for Jett to sit on a rock.

"What are we going to do? We need help, Tamblin. At the rate they are harvesting the Tasiers, there will be none left by the end of the month," Jett commented.

Tamblin looked up when he saw a fire flare up. The poachers were using long wands attached to tanks to burn the mushrooms. Their newest tactic helped to herd the Tasiers in the direction they wanted and forced his people into retreat since they had no place to hide.

"How far are they from Sandora?" Tamblin asked.

Jett winced when Tamblin pressed a cloth coated with a disinfectant against the cut on his forehead. "A week if they stay on their current course. If any more come or they spread out, it would take less time. Father and Mother have instructed the citizens of Sandora to move to the underground chambers," he confessed.

Tamblin frowned and shook his head. "Even that isn't safe, Jett. You heard them. Now that an alien is aware of our existence, he has set traps to capture us. Once he or one of the others finds the city, it will confirm what he has been telling them. Sandora will be destroyed," he said.

Jett nodded. "They will think of us as freaks and oddities to be sold and put on display for credits. I remember their joking comments," he bitterly stated.

He finished bandaging Jett's wound and packed the remains back into the kit. Jett murmured his thanks and stood. Tamblin could see the weariness in Jett's eyes. A sense of hopelessness threatened to overwhelm him when he saw the flames rising into the night sky and the thick plumes of smoke.

"We need help," he said.

"All we can do is hope that the sensors the Valdier placed have triggered an alert and they will come in time," Jett tiredly replied.

Tamblin pursed his lips. Even if the sensors were triggered, by the time the Valdier arrived, nothing would remain—including themselves.

"Jett, you need to convince your parents to evacuate Sandora to Glitter. We have the shields, the Guardians, and the protection of being buried deep within the mountain. Sandora is too vulnerable," he said in a hard voice.

There was no more time to debate the decision. Tamblin's brother-in-law stared out into the burning night with haunted eyes. There was no trace of the fun-loving man he used to know.

"I will tell them," Jett promised.

Three days later, Tamblin stood on the balcony watching as the last caravan of refugees from Sandora entered the cavern. The mood had been somber but filled with determination.

Construction crews from Glitter and Sandora continued to work around the clock, widening new sections of the cavern for the new arrivals. Merchants and farmers focused on giving each family supplies.

Roan, Jett's father and the King of Sandora, and Ladora, Jett's mother, guided their people to the finished levels. A movement from above caught Tamblin's attention, and he watched Batty release his grip from where he was hanging and fly down to the balcony, landing on the narrow railing. He chuckled when Batty lifted his chin and wiggled his nose.

"I don't think I've ever seen a bat this affectionate, especially after being around you for so long," Tia teased, walking up and standing beside him.

He started with surprise and lifted an eyebrow. "I didn't hear you come in," he said, frowning when he saw that she was alone. "Where are Jett and Arielle?"

Tia scratched Batty behind the ear. "Jett is helping his parents and Arielle is playing with some new friends. I needed to speak with you alone," she said.

"What's wrong?" he asked.

"I've had another vision," she confessed.

Tamblin's stomach clenched with worry. Batty nudged his hand, and he realized that he had threaded his fingers through the fine hair along Batty's neck. He forced his fingers to relax.

"What did you see?" he warily inquired.

She looked away from him to Batty. "You must go on a journey," she replied.

He stared at her with a confused expression. "A journey? Now? When our kingdoms... our very existence is in jeopardy?" he asked in a voice laced with skepticism.

Tia nodded and looked at him again. "Yes. It is the only way to save our world and our people," she answered.

"Tia." He shook his head. "Where am I supposed to go?" he asked.

She paused her stroking of Batty, and was silent for a moment.

"You have to find the Queen of the Wood Fairies," she finally said.

"Arosa? You are saying I have to find Arosa?" he repeated incredulously.

Tia turned emotion-filled eyes to him. He could see the truth of her conviction in them, but there was also something else. She looked—pensive.

"What aren't you telling me?" he quietly asked.

She reached for him. He gripped her hand, gently squeezing it in reassurance and studied her face. Tears glistened in her eyes. He pulled her into his arms and hugged her.

"I don't want you to get hurt, Tamblin," she whispered.

He pulled back and studied her face again. "Tell me what you saw," he instructed.

"Arosa has the power to save our world," she said in a slow, measured tone.

"But—" he added.

"But—she also has the power to hurt you," she replied.

He shook his head in denial. "Arosa would never hurt me. If she has the power to save our world, then I will find her and bring her back," he said in a confident voice.

"I know this is what must happen, but Tamblin—please be careful," Tia said.

Tamblin kissed her forehead, released her and stepped back. "I will. I'll find her, Tia," he reassured.

He motioned to Batty. The small mammal released his grip on the rail and launched into the air. Tamblin jumped up onto the railing and hopped onto the back of the hovering bat. He slid his feet into the stirrups, unwound the reins from the horn of the saddle, and looked at Tia. She stared back at him as if she wanted to say something more, but she raised her hand instead.

"I'll return as soon as possible," he promised, tapping Batty's sides.

"Be sure that you do!" she cried out behind him.

CHAPTER FOUR

Valdier:

Paul Grove looked up from the tablet he was reading when his wife, Morian, came out of the kitchen. There was a worried expression on her face. He placed the tablet aside.

"What's wrong?" he asked.

She looked at him with a crooked smile. "Have you noticed anything unusual this evening?" she inquired.

He frowned and looked around the living room. The coffee table had a variety of toys covering it. Crash, their symbiot, was sprawled out on the balcony. The aroma of cooking food made his stomach growl. Everything appeared normal. In fact, it was downright peaceful.

His eyes widened. "Morah," he muttered.

She chuckled and nodded. "I haven't seen her in almost an hour. By now she's usually at the table moaning about how she is starving and we never feed her," she replied.

"I better check on her," he laughed as he got up from his chair.

"Tell her dinner will be in ten minutes," she called after him.

He scooped up several of his daughter's dolls as he walked down the hallway. Turning the toys in his hands, he shook his head. His oldest daughter, Trisha, had played with soldiers—real life ones. They were polar opposites about some things.

"But the same in others," he chuckled, looking at the princess doll in the flowing gown wearing a laser pistol at her hip.

He paused outside of his daughter's door and frowned when he saw it was closed. Morah never closed her door. He reached out and gripped the doorknob. The door was locked.

Surprised, he listened. He could hear her talking. He gently knocked on the door.

"Morah, honey, unlock the door," he said.

"I busy, Daddy," Morah called through the closed door.

Paul frowned and looked at the door with a raised eyebrow. "Busy?" he repeated to himself.

He knocked on the door again. "Morah, can you open the door, please. Mommy said dinner is almost ready. You need to get cleaned up," he replied.

"I can't eats right now. I'm busy," Morah responded.

He studied the door and wondered what was going on. Morah was talking again but obviously not to him. Curious, he pressed his ear to the door.

"You in loves. I know becauses my mommy and daddy has that weirds look in their eyes too when they talk about each others," Morah was saying.

Paul pulled back and gripped the doorknob again. "Morah, who is in there with you?" he demanded.

He stepped back when the door knob rattled. His eyes widened when his petite daughter scowled up at him with a disapproving air. He tried to peer inside her room, but she pulled the door partially closed behind herself so he couldn't.

"I is having a meeting, Daddy. This is importants. It is about loves and wishes. I can't eats dinner yet," she explained in a very serious tone.

Paul studied Morah. She was wearing a pair of oversized golden glasses—without any lens in the frames—one of his white dress shirts unbuttoned down the front, and a name tag with… He tilted his head to read it, Dr. Morah, written in uneven, childish lettering.

"Dr. Morah?" he asked with a raised eyebrow.

She reached up and adjusted her fake glasses and nodded. "The Goddess needs helps. I tolds her if she ever needs helps I would gives it to her. We's having an… inner… inner… a session," she announced with an emphatic nod of her head.

Paul reached out and steadied the tall, pointed princess hat that tilted sideways from her movement. He tried looking into the room again, but Morah pushed a hand against his stomach. He cleared his throat and looked down at her.

"Are you saying you have one of the Goddesses in your bedroom, and you are having an intervention session with her?" he asked.

He wanted to clarify what he was going to tell Morian.

"Yes—and you is interruptings us," Morah pointed out.

"My apologies. I'll let Mommy know you'll be busy for a bit longer," he replied, trying not to laugh.

"Thank you, Daddy," she replied.

She began to close the door before she paused, sniffed the air, looked down the hallway, then turned eyes filled with longing up to him. He could see the conflict on her face. The sound of her tummy rumbling gave her thoughts away.

"How about I bring you a plate—or two. After all, counseling a Goddess is hard work, and I imagine both of you are probably hungry," he suggested.

Morah's face lit up with delight, and she wrapped her arms around his legs. He adjusted her hat again when she pulled back and looked up at him with a smile. He bent down and kissed her forehead.

"I'll put a tray outside the door," he murmured.

"You are the best Daddy evers," she whispered back to him.

As she went back into her bedroom and closed the door, he frowned. Why would a Goddess need help with love issues? More importantly—what was Morah telling her? He jumped with a start when a slender arm wrapped around his waist.

"Is everything alright?" Morian asked, resting her chin against his arm.

"Sometimes I feel very old," he replied with a sigh.

Morian laughed and shook her head. "Trust me when I say I'm the one who robbed the cradle," she teased before she looked at the door and continued, "Please tell me she isn't plotting to take over the world."

He shook his head. "No. She is going to need a tray with dinner for two," he replied, sliding his arm around her as they both walked back to the living room.

"Two?" she inquired with a surprised expression.

He nodded. "It would appear that she is now Dr. Morah, counselor to the Goddesses," he chuckled.

Morian glanced up at him in surprise before looking back over her shoulder. Her lips were parted, and her eyes were wide, so he couldn't resist kissing her.

"Oh my," she replied with a laugh.

"Yes. I suspect this is only the beginning. I'll make her a tray," he said with a shake of his head.

Arosa looked at the little girl as she adjusted the gold, symbiot-created glasses on her nose. Morah smoothed down the white shirt she wore over a glittering pink gown as she resumed her seat on the pink bench.

Arosa wondered for the thousandth time if she should have come here. It had been an impulsive decision to come visit the Valdier palace. She was searching for answers and hoped that perhaps seeing how the older Valdier interacted would give her some guidance.

Instead, she felt more confused than ever. The longing inside her grew stronger as she watched the couples laughing, kissing, and talking with each other. Those moments reminded her of her evening with Tamblin. With still no response from Aikaterina or Arilla, she had sought the only other person who she thought could help her—Morah.

"Okays, where weres we?" Morah asked.

"You were explaining that what I was feeling is love," Arosa replied from where she was lying on Morah's bed.

Morah nodded, almost toppling her princess hat. "Okays. Buttercup, you takes notes this times," she instructed.

Arosa gave the little girl a faint smile when she looked at the symbiot over the rim of her glasses. Buttercup was laying on the floor in the shape of a rabbit. There was a child's tablet lying between the symbiot's paws. Buttercup wiggled her nose and sniffed the tablet.

I think I'm glad that Arilla can't see me now, Arosa ruefully thought.

"Okays, does the Kings of the Leprechaun's makes you mad?" Morah asked.

Arosa frowned and began to sit up. She stopped when Morah gave her a pointed look and shook her head. Leaning back and relaxing against the pile of pillows again, she demurely folded her hands like Morah had instructed earlier and shook her head.

"No. Should he?" she asked.

"Onlys if yous in love like Aunty Riley or likes Springs. They is always threatenings to buries a body. Spring could do it becauses she likes to digs holes. Maybes I should tell Aunty Riley she needs to talks to Spring," Morah responded, tapping a finger to her chin.

"Is that the only way to know if what you feel for someone is love?" Arosa inquired.

Morah shook her head. "No. My mommy and daddy loves each others a lots. They have a quiets love. I thinks that is the kinds of love that you and the Leprechaun has," she decided.

"What do you suggest I do?" Arosa asked.

Morah stood up and walked over to her. She watched with growing apprehension as Morah held her hand and looked at her with a solemn expression. Worried, she sat up.

"You's gots to go to him. Loves is what makes the worlds go round," she said in a low, determined tone.

"But—what do I tell him when he finds out that I'm not really the Queen of the Wood Fairies?" Arosa asked in a hushed voice.

"If he's loves you, it won't matters. My daddy didn't cares that my mommy was a dragon. He loves her because she's my mommy," Morah declared.

Arosa frowned. She wasn't sure it was the same thing—but maybe it was. She lifted a hand to her chest. The strange beating was there again, along with a fluttering in her stomach. Both feelings were alien to her.

"I'll go," she said.

Morah reached over and hugged her. "Don't forgets to tells him the truth. Mommy says if you tells the truth, he's gots to forgive you," she added.

Arosa nodded. "I will. Thank you for your guidance, Little Priestess," she replied.

"Are you hungrys? My daddy was making us some dinner," Morah said.

Arosa shook her head. "No, thank you. I have a few things to do before I go," she said.

"Do you minds if I eat all of your foods? I's starving," Morah said, rubbing her tummy.

"It would be a shame for it to go to waste," she teased.

"Oh, I forgots something! You needs a pretty dress. I have lots of pretty dresses," Morah exclaimed.

Arosa wanted to protest, but the excitement on Morah's face was too much for her tender heart to decline. Ten minutes later, she clutched a beautiful green and silver doll gown to her chest and stepped through an opening back to the Hive.

She solidified and walked along the path, rolling the silky material of the doll gown between her fingers. She looked around the long cavern. While others who came here saw rough stone and boulders, it was an illusion.

She waved her hand and a ripple of gold flowed outward, revealing her home. She brushed her fingers against the polished marble statues of different beings from many places in the universe. The statues moved under her touch. The polished marble floor had designs of different star systems embedded.

She smiled when she saw a new image forming. It reminded her of the power of her species. Young symbiots lounged along the River of Life that streamed out into space through the large Gateway. She looked up at the ceiling. Brilliant colorful ribbons of stars, planets, and nebulas floated overhead.

Along each side, rows of pillars held up the arched ceiling and no longer looked worn or crumbling. The smooth, cream-colored surfaces were now unblemished with age. Behind the columns , unseen by others, were alcoves that gave privacy to those that visited and those that lived here.

She walked over to her own alcove where she enjoyed creating replicas of worlds and the creatures who she imagined would one day live on them. She traced her fingers over the current model she was working on. She smiled when she realized it was very similar to Valdier.

She looked at the table next to the chaise lounge where she had placed an ornate symbiot bracelet with the etchings of a bat in flight. The symbiot was pulsing with light. She hurried over to it and picked up the bracelet.

"Show me," she requested.

Flashes of images poured through the symbiot to her. "Tamblin," she breathed when she saw his tired face.

The symbiot tied to Batty shared the struggle against the poachers. Arosa trembled when she saw time after time Tamblin barely escaping from the traps set by the larger men. She closed her eyes.

"I can't look the other way and ignore them," she whispered.

She retraced her steps to the main cavern. Impatient, she dissolved and soared across to the star chart for Tamblin's small moon. She activated the appropriate gateway and floated up to the platform.

"I'm coming, Tamblin," she said, stepping through the gateway.

CHAPTER FIVE

The Minor Moon of Leviathan:

"Batty!" Tamblin yelled as the small bat tumbled from the sky.

He tightened his grip on the saddle as they spiraled downward. He could smell the pungent scent of burned hair. The tiny bat struggled to right himself.

Tamblin cursed when a rock wall came into view in front of them. Batty frantically flapped his wings, but they slammed into the wall. The impact knocked the rider from his perch.

He clung to the saddle, his feet dangling as they slid down the rock face. Tamblin lost his tenuous hold on the saddle when Batty used his thumbs to grip a narrow crevice in the rock.

For a brief second, he was weightless until his feet connected with a ledge. He teetered backwards, his arms flailing outward as he tried to keep his balance. He looked over his shoulder and swallowed. While the ledge he stood on might not be very high for a poacher, it was deadly to someone his size. He twisted and pressed his back against the rock wall behind him.

"I think I got one of them," a man shouted.

Adrenaline poured through him when a bright light flashed in his direction. He crouched down and blindly felt behind him. There was a wide crack in the rock. He slid into it just as the light flashed by him again, illuminating the darkness.

Right inside the entrance there was a hollowed out area. He ducked into it, crouching to keep from hitting his head. The sound of heavy footsteps came closer. He reached down and pulled a knife from his boot.

"Anything yet, Harron?" a man asked.

"No. I could have sworn I hit the creature. Help me find it," Harron replied.

Tamblin flattened his body as far as he could in the narrow gap. A light slowly flashed over the rock. Light danced across the opening, giving him a better view of the cave. It was deeper than he'd expected, going back several feet before widening.

He inhaled a swift breath when the light focused on the crevice where he was hiding. A dirty hand, almost as wide as he was tall, appeared. Tamblin tightened his grip on the knife in his hand.

His breathing grew shallow when long, thick fingers felt around the interior. As long as the man didn't curl his fingers, he should be safe. The man cursed when a jagged piece of rock along the ceiling sliced his flesh. The man would have been able to remove his hand again if he hadn't twisted it.

"What's wrong?" the other man asked.

"My hand's stuck," Harron growled.

"Well, you should have known better than to stick it in there. There's no telling what kind of poisonous creatures might live in the rocks," the other man said with a snicker of amusement.

"Shut up and help me pull my arm out," Harron snapped.

Tamblin lifted an arm to protect his head from falling debris as Harron yanked his arm free. He listened to the two men mutter to each other. Only when the light moved away did he lean his head back and take a deep, calming breath. He stiffly climbed out of his hiding place and stood.

He was taking a step forward when he noticed a movement out of the corner of his eye. He jerked back with a muttered oath, then a soft chuckle of relief slipped from him when Batty peered in the crevice opening at him. The wily creature wiggled until he was through the crack.

"Come, let me look at your wound," he softly instructed.

Remorse filled Tamblin when Batty limped by him to the back of the cave. He followed. He ran his hand along Batty's side to the buckle of the saddle and quickly removed it along with the harness.

Feeling inside the saddlebag, he pulled out a small expanding staff. With a twist, the red gem on the end began to glow. In the light, he could see the dark streak of blood along the bat's side.

He propped the staff up against the wall and reached inside the bag once more, pulling out a small medical kit. He cleaned the wound, whispering soothing words when Batty squeaked in pain. The medicine numbed the area and would prevent infection.

"Thank you, my young friend. If not for you, I would never have seen those men," he confessed.

Batty nudged Tamblin with his head. Compassion filled him when Batty's eyes drooped with fatigue. They both needed some rest. It would be light in a few hours. Although that would make it easier for him to see, it would restrict Batty—and make it more dangerous to travel by air.

He looked up at the ceiling and back down at Batty. "Get some rest," he ordered.

Batty nodded and pushed off the floor of the cavern. He watched the bat gracefully twist in the air and clutch the ceiling with his feet, hanging upside down. In seconds, Batty had wrapped his wings around his body and was sound asleep.

Tamblin returned the items to the bag, sheathed his knife, and walked to the entrance of the cave. He stood there for some time, silently scanning the area. In the distance, he could see the poachers' lights moving away. Depression hit him hard.

"How will we ever win against such odds?" he wondered out loud.

Tia had said that Arosa could help them—but how? Even if she had an army, it would be no match against the poachers and their machines. A shudder ran through him when he remembered the size of the man's hand. One squeeze and the poacher could crush him. He didn't want to think of the damage the man could do to someone as delicate as Arosa.

He looked back into the cave. If he continued on, he might make it to the forest before the end of the day. His decision made, he returned to the back of the cave. He packed a smaller bag with a few essentials and pulled the strap over his head.

Batty's squeak caused him to look up. Large brown and gold eyes gaze down at him with an accusing expression. A wave of remorse swept through him. It was obvious Batty thought he was abandoning him.

"I will continue on. Find me when nightfall comes again. I want you healthy and well-rested," he gently instructed, picking up the staff.

Batty wiggled his nose and blinked in response before nodding and covering his head with his wing again. With his guilt slightly eased, Tamblin tightened the strap to the bag on his back and strode back to the opening. He took a deep breath and began descending the rock face. He still had a long, treacherous journey ahead of him.

Arosa solidified on the edge of the rock shelf in front of a dark cave. Her symbiot connection with the young bat had guided her to his location. Behind her, the sun was rising above the horizon.

"Tamblin," she called, stepping up to the cave's entrance. She lifted a hand and a golden light filtered from it into the opening. "Tamblin, are you hurt?" she anxiously asked, hurrying forward.

She stopped when she saw the saddle. She peered up at the ceiling. Batty unfurled his wings, yawned, and looked down at her with sleepy eyes.

"Batty, where is Tamblin?" she asked in an urgent tone.

She floated up to the bat and caressed his head with a gentle hand. Her breath caught when she sensed Batty's pain. The bat looked at her with sad eyes.

"Show me," she coaxed.

Batty lifted his left wing, showing her a long burn, blistered and red, on his side. She ran her hand along the wound. The flesh sealed and fine, dark brown hair grew as she caressed the damaged area. She murmured soothing words when the small bat trembled.

"Where is Tamblin?" she asked.

"I will continue on. Find me when nightfall comes again. I want you healthy and well-rested." Tamblin's deep voice echoed through her mind.

"No!" she cried, looking back toward the crevice opening.

Twirling, she floated out of the cavern. Power flowed through her as her fear for Tamblin grew. She reached out, connecting with every living being—both plant and animal. A vision of Tamblin appeared. He was running, and she noticed the lines under the ground moving behind him —sandworms.

She burst forward and in a matter of seconds, she located him. The ground under his feet rose, sending him flying. He hit the ground and rolled, coming up onto his feet with a long staff in his hand. He swung around as three sandworms broke through the surface and surrounded him.

She opened her arms, shifting into the Wood Fairy Queen, and wrapped her arms around his waist from behind. She lifted him off the ground as two of the sandworms struck, flying up to the top of a mushroom, and released him. Turning in midair, she swept her hands outward. The sandworms' bodies rippled as they began to change. Their bodies became stems, and their open mouths turned into dark red flowers with yellow and orange centers.

"Arosa!" Tamblin exclaimed in shock, sheathing his sword.

"A beast is coming. It isn't safe for you out in the open," she said.

She swept her arms around him again and lifted him off the mushroom, depositing him onto the ground. He gripped her hand, and they ran through the maze of mushrooms—until the ground suddenly gave way under his feet.

Arosa twisted when Tamblin's hand unexpectedly ripped away from hers. She realized that a sandworm tunnel had opened under his feet. Terror gripped her when he disappeared. She faded again, reappearing next to him as he fell.

She wrapped her arms around him, and with a thought, a thick pile of soft spores appeared under them. They landed on the cushioned floor of the tunnel. The impact forced them apart.

"Arosa, are you alright?" Tamblin urgently asked.

She sat up and sneezed. She lifted her eyes to his and choked back a giggle. A dusting of fine, rainbow-colored particles covered Tamblin from head to foot.

"I'm fine. Are you hurt?" she asked, grasping his hand when he held it out.

He grimaced when he saw his clothing. "Only my pride," he chuckled, brushing the colorful powder off of his clothing.

They both looked up when the ground shook and pieces of dirt rained down. Tamblin lifted her out of the pile of spores, pulled her away from the opening, and held her in his arms. She pressed against him and looked over her shoulder.

"Did the beast find something this time, Macron?" a man shouted.

"Maybe. There's a hole," Macron answered.

Arosa looked at Tamblin. He shook his head. She pressed her face against him when the sound of savage snarling reverberated around them. The snarls were followed by a cascade of dirt as the ground was ripped opened. Long, sharp claws dug at the soil. The beast was enlarging the hole they had fallen through.

"This way," Tamblin murmured near her ear.

CHAPTER SIX

Once he determined it was safe, Tamblin twisted the crystal at top of his staff. Its red glow lit the sandworm tunnel. The last thing he wanted to do was to run face first into one of those beasts. He was conscious of Arosa's tight grip on the back of his coat.

"Where are we going?" she inquired.

He glanced over his shoulder before focusing on where he was going. It was a good thing he did because he would have run face first into a long root hanging from the tunnel ceiling. He reached out and pushed it out of the way, holding it back until Arosa passed through.

"We are searching for another way out," he explained.

He stopped and looked up when the ground above them shook. The loud sound of a creature sniffing sent a shiver through him. He reached back and gripped Arosa's hand, pulling her quickly behind him when the creature growled.

When the tunnel collapsed, they were only a few feet away. From the opening above, light poured in, and a narrow beige-colored snout appeared. Long, sharp teeth protruded from the beast's mouth, and the creature's massive claws tore at the ground.

"Macron, call your beast off! At the rate it's going, we're going to have a trench, and it will have eaten anything worth selling," a poacher snapped in irritation.

"Shut up, Harron. If we want to make this trip worthwhile, we're going to need more than the Tasiers. We'll be lucky if we get enough credits to pay for the fuel for this disaster, and if the Dragon Lords find out what we're doing, we'll be lucky to make it out of here alive. You saw the sensors. If the blockers we put on them fail and it sends out a report, we're dead," Macron retorted.

"What are they trying to do?" Arosa asked.

Tamblin paused when the tunnel forked. He lifted the staff and looked at each tunnel before he turned to the right. He kept a tight grip on Arosa's hand as they moved farther away from the poachers and their beast.

"Tia had a vision that the poachers would return to our moon. My security teams sighted the first of them a few weeks ago. They set out traps to capture the Tasiers," he explained, stopping to look up at one narrow hole.

"But—the Valdier have declared this moon under their protection," she protested.

Tamblin nodded. "Yes, but they aren't here. Our hope was the sensors the Valdier scientists installed would trigger an alert and bring help, but as you just heard, the poachers have blocked them," he replied, continuing along the passage.

"Why are they trying to capture you? You are not a Tasier," she demanded.

He stopped and faced her. In the staff's glow, he could see the worry and confusion on her face. He brushed a smudge of dirt from her cheek.

"We have been trying to disable their ships and release Tasiers from their traps for the past month," he said.

"Oh, Tamblin, I'm so sorry," she replied, cupping his hand against her cheek.

He shook his head. "For the first few days, we were success-ful, but the poachers soon discovered there was something amiss. They repaired their ships almost as fast as we could sabotage them. Then they set traps for us. Several warriors were injured, and we almost lost a team when they became trapped on board a transport. Jett and Santil freed them at the last second. We continued releasing the Tasiers, but even that became too hazardous to do during the daylight hours. For the next couple of weeks, squadrons worked at night, but the poachers upgraded the locking mechanisms. We could no longer open the traps as quickly as before. Then, a creature like the one we encountered back there caught one of our soldiers—and nearly killed him. We rescued him but not before a poacher saw us. Now, those two hunt us as much as they do the Tasiers. Roan, King of Sandora, and I have both sent scouts out to warn other kingdoms," he said.

"And you came looking for me," she replied.

"Yes. Everyone on the moon is in danger, including the Wood Fairies. I wanted to find you earlier, to find out why you disappeared the next morning without saying goodbye—It doesn't matter. I shouldn't have brought that up now." He looked away from her.

"Tamblin—"

"We'd best keep moving," he said, walking away.

He tried to ignore the hurt in her eyes. He was just trying to protect his own heart from being hurt again. Her disappearance the morning after their night together had been like a dagger to his heart. She had vanished, leaving nothing behind but a note attached to Batty.

"Tamblin," she called from behind him.

He slowed his pace, realizing he had been so focused on his thoughts that he wasn't paying attention. He took a deep breath and faced her. He frowned when she didn't walk toward him.

"What?" he asked in a tone sharper than he meant. "I'm sorry, Arosa. What is it?"

She pointed to a tunnel. His frown deepened, and he walked over to her. The passage made a gradual incline and opened at the base of an outcropping of rocks.

"I thought this might be a good exit," she softly replied.

He cleared his throat and nodded. "Yes, it's perfect. I'll go first to make sure it's safe," he said.

Arosa stared at Tamblin's back with longing. She had created the tunnel, knowing it would give them safe passage to the surface. Lifting the hem of her dress, she followed him at a slower pace.

Remorse filled her. He was hurt by her sudden disappearance that night, of course he was. She hadn't known how to handle all the unfamiliar emotions sweeping through her then, and she still didn't.

What future could we ever have? she thought.

"It's safe," he said, holding out his hand to her.

She placed her hand in his and climbed up the steep incline. He helped her out of the hole, and they scrambled to hide behind the rocks. A hundred yards away, two large poachers stood talking while a hairless mammal with a long and wrinkled snout, beady black eyes, and stubby ears clawed at the ground. The beast's head disappeared in the hole and when it reemerged, a torn piece of her gown hung from between its teeth.

A man's shout of triumph split the air as he yanked the cloth from the beast's mouth. He waved it in the other man's face. She and Tamblin ducked their heads when the man looked around.

"I told you I saw something!" Macron chortled.

Harron grabbed the material and turned it over in his hand before he tossed it back at Macron. "That's a dress for a doll," he retorted in disgust.

"Hey now, do you see any kids around here? I'm telling you it belongs to those creatures that are sabotaging our ships and releasing the Tasiers," Macron argued.

"The only one who saw something was you, and I made the mistake of believing your wild tales. We need to focus on the Tasiers. We haven't lost any more of them since we upgraded the locks on the traps—that *I* purchased, I might add. How do I know you aren't trying to jeopardize this business endeavor?" Harron sneered.

Macron grabbed Harron by the collar, and the two men struggled for a few minutes. Arosa stared at the conflict with a combination of awe and horror. She jumped when Tamblin wrapped his fingers around her arm.

"Why are they fighting with each other?" she asked.

Tamblin frowned. "Because that is what they do," he replied.

She lifted the hem of the green and silver gown Morah had given her and followed him as he climbed. She gazed up at the mountain of rocks. This was a lot more work than she'd expected.

"Where are we going?" she asked with a sigh.

Tamblin stopped and looked over his shoulder at her. "First, we are going to find a place where we are safe. Then, we are going to head back to my kingdom," he explained, resuming his climb.

"But—why are we heading north if your kingdom is to the east?" she asked.

He stopped. She stared at his stiff frame. His shoulders rose and fell as if he were taking a deep breath, holding it, and then releasing it.

"I was coming to find you because Tia said you had the power to save our world—and she is never wrong. Now, we are returning to the cave where I left Batty, which is north of here," he replied.

Arosa swayed with shock. "Tia told you about me?" she asked.

Tamblin looked over his shoulder at her again and frowned. "I told her that unless you have an army we don't know about, I find it very unlikely that you can help us, but I have a duty to my people to try anything I can to save them. If you can turn the poachers into flowers the way you did the sandworms, that would work," he replied with a raised eyebrow.

She shook her head. "I—can't," she said, biting her lip.

He sighed. "Well, I guess that was too much to hope for. We'd better move. Once they finish beating each other up, they'll start searching for us again," he replied.

Arosa nodded, not that Tamblin saw the movement. He had already turned around and started climbing again. She tried to follow him, but her feet kept slipping on the loose gravel.

She sighed and looked down at her feet. This terrain required more practical footwear than the slippers she was wearing. In the blink of an eye, the dainty slippers were transformed into a pair of sturdy hiking boots. She lifted the gown and secured it with a wide, golden belt that appeared around her waist.

With a flutter of her wings, she rose off the ground. Tamblin was a fair distance from her now, and flying would be the fastest—and easiest—way to catch up with him.

As soon as she was close to him, she squeaked in surprise when he swiftly turned, wrapped his arm around her waist, and pulled her down against his body. She tried to speak, but he covered her mouth with his hand and stared over her shoulder. He muttered a curse and frantically searched the area around them.

"Stay quiet. They are coming this way," he warned, pulling her down until she was crouching beside him.

She nodded when he moved his hand. He kept his arms wrapped around her as they peered between the rocks. Her flight up to Tamblin must have attracted the men's attention.

"You busted my nose," Macron growled, wiping the blood off with the sleeve of his shirt.

"You bit me," Harron retorted. "What is it?"

Macron stopped a few feet from Tamblin and Arosa. "I saw something," he remarked in a distracted voice.

Tamblin held her tighter when Macron took another step closer. Arosa narrowed her eyes and focused on the ground. Hundreds of small butterflies rose from the mushrooms and swarmed around the two men. She lifted her hand and smothered her giggles when the men jumped back with startled yells.

When she looked at the hairless beast, she noticed that it was staring in their direction. A mischievous smile curved her lips.

Do not hunt the Tasiers or the people of this moon any longer. They are under my protection, she instructed.

The hairless beast bowed its head. It turned, looked at the two men dancing in frantic circles before it took off in the direction of the ships. The men soon followed the beast. Satisfied with her ploy, she leaned back and beamed when Tamblin softly chuckled in her ear.

"Maybe this is why Tia said I needed to find you," he mused.

"Why is that?" she asked, looking at him.

She caught her breath when their lips nearly touched. She stared into his eyes as a heightened sense of awareness flooded her. He tightened his hold on her.

"Luck—perhaps you will bring us luck," he replied.

She parted her lips and leaned into him, hoping he would kiss her. Disappointment quickly replaced anticipation when he rose to his feet, pulling her up with him. He released her and stepped back.

"We'd better go. It will take us a few days to get back to Glitter. A laser blast hit Batty. I left him in a cave a half day's journey from here. If possible, I'd like to get back to him before dark," he said, avoiding her eyes.

She silently nodded, not bothering to hide the hurt caused by his rejection. Instead, she followed him down the rocks to the ground. It didn't seem necessary to inform him that Batty was safe and his wounds now healed. He would discover that when they reached the cave.

CHAPTER SEVEN

Tamblin paused and looked over his shoulder at Arosa. She wiped her damp brow and gave him a quivering smile. He looked away from her and scanned the area.

"We can take a break here," he said.

She silently followed him. He stopped under an enormous red and yellow mushroom with soft white gills. Dozens of smaller mushrooms grew under the protective umbrella of the larger one. He shrugged off his coat and covered the top of one of the smaller mushrooms.

"You can sit here. This way you won't ruin your dress," he offered.

"Thank you, but I think it is a little late for that," she ruefully replied, fingering a long tear in the green material.

A surge of shame over his behavior threatened to swallow him. He'd spent the last two hours fluctuating between wanting to wrap his arms around her and being a total jerk. It happened that being a total jerk had won.

She swept her damp hair back and sighed, pointedly looking at everything except him. He placed his pack on the ground and retrieved his water bottle. He shook it, muttering under his breath when he realized it was empty.

"Do you need water?" she asked.

He nodded. "We need water. It is important we stay hydrated," he replied as he stood.

She worried her bottom lip. "If you like, I can—"

He shook his head. "I've got this," he interrupted and removed the knife from his boot.

She loudly sighed and became quiet again. He looked around the area, sending up a silent thank you to the Goddesses when he saw the flat, ruffled texture of a milk-white Dragon's Beard mushroom.

The Dragon's Beard would not only give them plenty of water, but its meat was sweet, delicious, and nutritious. He walked over to the plant and poked a small hole in it with his knife. Clear water poured from it into the bottle. When it was full, he cut a small section off the tip of the mushroom.

In seconds, a thin film covered the cut section, sealing off the flow of water and protecting the mushroom. He carried the mushroom piece and the water back to Arosa and held out the bottle. She gave him a brief smile before she took the offered bottle of water.

"Thank you," she said.

He studied her when she stared at the bottle before sniffing it. An amused smile tugged at his lips when she finally took a drink. She seemed almost surprised by the cool liquid. She drank deeply before sighing again.

"There is plenty more," he assured her.

She shook her head and offered him the bottle. "You have some first. You have been traveling longer than I," she insisted.

He took the bottle and sat down beside her. Placing the bottle between his legs, he tore the piece of mushroom and handed half of it to her. She fingered the soft white meat before pinching off a section and placing it in her mouth.

"This is good," she remarked with surprise.

"Do you not have Dragon's Beard in your forest?" he asked before breaking off a section and eating it.

"This type of fungi is found on many planets, though they call it different names. Aik—" she started to explain before she stopped and looked at the piece in her hand. "It is very good," she finished lamely.

"How did you find me earlier?" he suddenly asked.

She choked on a small piece of mushroom she was eating and coughed. He patted her on the back and handed her the water bottle. She took a deep swig and cleared her throat.

"I… the butterflies warned that there was a disturbance and I…uh…came to investigate," she haltingly answered.

"I'm thankful that you did. It was interesting how you could do that—turn the sandworms into flowers," he reflected.

"It… as the Queen of the Wood Fairies, I have a certain skill when it comes to plants. The sandworms weren't harmed. The flowers grew around them," she said with a wave of her hand.

"Fascinating," he murmured.

"It is? Yes, it is," she hastily corrected.

He wanted to ask her one more question that was puzzling him—*why had she left him without saying goodbye the morning after*—but he was afraid of the answer. There was a lot he wanted to say, but an awkward silence fell between them as they finished their simple meal. He offered her the bottle again.

"No, thank you," she said, wiping the mushroom crumbs off her dress.

"I'll refill the water bottle and cut another section off the mushroom just in case we need it later. It tastes better roasted. We should get going if we want to make it back to Batty by nightfall. I told him to find me, but I don't know if he understood. He might end up back at the palace," he mused.

"He understood," she replied.

She looked so certain he couldn't help asking, "How can you be certain?"

She gave him that mysterious smile of hers and slid off the mushroom. "Bats are very smart creatures," she replied with a confident nod.

"Well, I think we should still try to get back to the cave. If nothing else, it will give us protection. The poachers are more active at night," he said.

He refilled the water bottle and cut off another piece of the mushroom. She held his bag and coat while he stored their meager supplies. The tiny frown line between her eyes made him smile. She was watching everything he did as if it were all new to her.

Her soft cheek was smudged with dirt. He took his coat from her and pulled a handkerchief from the pocket. Dampening one end with the trickle of water still dripping from the mushroom, he gently wiped the spot.

"Tamblin," she whispered, looking at him, her eyes filled with longing and confusion.

He caressed her cheek with his thumb. "We'd better go," he quietly responded.

After several stops, they reached the bottom of the rock face where he had left Batty just before dusk. The last couple of hours had been the most taxing. He had pushed not only himself but Arosa at an exhausting pace. His biggest motivation was fear for her. The thought of her being exposed to the horrors of the poachers superseded everything else.

He held out his hand. "Just a little farther, we are almost there," he promised.

She grasped his hand and stepped up beside him on a rock. "I can take us the rest of the way," she offered.

The protest on his lips died when she wrapped her arms around him. She looked up at the opening, and when he looked up too, his feet left the ground. Her wings fluttered so quickly he barely saw them. In seconds, they were on the ledge from where he had descended nearly fourteen hours earlier.

"Thank—thank you," he said when she released him.

She self-consciously pushed a lock of her hair back and gave him a shy smile. "You're welcome," she replied before walking past him into the cave.

He followed her with his gaze until she disappeared from sight. He sighed and looked behind him at the horizon. Bright spotlights and the unmistakably gray clouds of smoke created a glowing haze along the skyline.

Hopelessness filled him as he stared out at the devastation. These men cared nothing about the lives they were destroying. Their only concern was for the credits they would earn.

Tia, I fear nothing short of a Goddess can save our world this time, he thought with despair.

CHAPTER EIGHT

Arosa glanced over her shoulder before studying the cave in front of her. Batty peeked down at her and gave her a toothy grin at the changes she made to the drab interior. All day she had fought against the urge to make things easier for Tamblin.

Even so, she might have been responsible for the Dragon Beard mushrooms appearing when they needed water... and because of her, no sandworms tried to attack them. Also, there had been a cooling breeze that stayed with them, there were fewer obstacles to block their way, and heavy rain had kept the poachers from the area.

Now she focused on making the night more pleasant. The cave expanded. In the corner, a deep oval depression formed. Water poured down along the wall from a crack and filled the area, then the torrent became a continuous trickle. In another corner, dried wood appeared. There would be enough firewood for several nights.

Batty squeaked in appreciation. She sent him a mischievous glance and lifted a finger to her lips. She smiled and the ceiling of the cave came alive with glowing green lights from iridescent glow worms.

"Don't eat them. They are merely an illusion," she cautioned.

Tamblin would need something to sleep on—but what could she add that would look natural? She worried her bottom lip as she scanned the area. An idea formed, and long, soft curly moss grew down from the ceiling, forming thick clumps next to the pool of water. The moss flowed outward until it created a level area on the floor.

This will work, she decided with satisfaction.

Batty squeaked again and landed next to her. She scratched behind his ear when he pressed his head against her side.

Tamblin stepped into the larger section of the cavern and Batty's eyes lit up with pleasure. Tamblin affectionately murmured to Batty when he scurried over to Tamblin with a joyous squeak.

"He missed you," she teased.

Tamblin chuckled and stroked Batty. "He *is* an affectionate creature. I've never seen one behave like this," he admitted. He looked around the cavern. "I don't remember the cave looking like this before."

"You said it was dark when you left," she reminded him.

The confusion in his eyes faded, and he nodded. "True. I'll admit I'm glad it is much nicer than I remembered," he confessed.

"Batty can keep watch for us. I believe I saw some wood in the corner. Do you have a way to light a fire?" she asked.

Tamblin nodded and frowned again. "I must have been more exhausted or distracted than I realized. I know Batty was hurt. I remember applying salve to his wound, but there's no mark. Even his hair has grown back," he mused.

She nervously shifted when Tamblin ran his hand along the bat's side where he'd been wounded. Batty looked at her with wide eyes, as if trying to decide if he should squeak in pain. She frantically nodded, trying not to laugh when Batty over-dramatized his pain, fell over onto his other side, and covered his head with his wing.

"On second thought, maybe he's hurt worse than I realized," Tamblin said.

"If you'd like to start a fire, I will tend to Batty," she offered.

He reluctantly nodded. "I hope he doesn't have any broken ribs."

"I'm sure he is fine. Perhaps a little sore still," she reassured him.

She flashed Tamblin a brief, encouraging smile when he nodded again and walked away. Batty peeked at her from under his wing. She barely smothered her chuckle of amusement when she noticed the mischievous delight reflected in the bat's eyes and he winked.

"Thank you," she murmured.

She distractedly stroked Batty's side while she watched Tamblin work. He was meticulous. He thought out each of his movements before he did them, paying attention to every detail.

Before long, he had a fire burning in a small pit. She was curious when she noticed that he anchored two sticks in the pile of rocks until he pulled out the remaining pieces of mushroom from his bag. He washed them before skewering and securing them over the fire to roast.

"He makes doing the simplest things fascinating," she mused.

As if he heard her, he looked up and their eyes connected. Her hand skimmed along Batty's wing as she took a step, then two toward Tamblin. Batty, sensing it was time to go, rolled to his feet and scurried toward the cave entrance.

"If you'd like to get cleaned up, dinner will be ready soon," Tamblin informed her.

"What about you?" she asked.

He chuckled. "It wouldn't hurt for me to get cleaned up as well," he acknowledged.

"Good," she said, reaching for him.

She covered his lips with hers in a passionate kiss. He stiffened with surprise and then moaned as he wrapped his arms around her. The hammering in her chest increased and excitement coursed through her.

"Arosa," he groaned, kissing her neck.

"Yes, Tamblin. Yes," she replied, unfastening his shirt.

An hour later, Tamblin kissed Arosa's bare shoulder where her gown had slipped down. Memories of the magic they had just created in the shallow pool burned through his mind, making him hungry for more. Her giggle caused him to smile.

"We're lucky the food didn't burn," he said, handing her one of the sticks with a section of the roasted mushroom on it.

"Yes, we are," she responded.

"Why did you leave?" he suddenly asked, sitting down across from her.

She gave him a startled look and lowered her eyes. He watched a variety of expressions cross her face as she thought about how to answer him. She picked at the mushroom.

"Tamblin, there is something I should have told you," she began.

The sound of Batty's frantic squeaking interrupted her. He placed his meal aside and stood, grabbing his shirt and pulling it on as he hurried to the entrance of the cave. The bright glow of fires stretched out to the horizon. The acrid stench of smoke filled the air. Fastening his shirt, he skidded to a stop beside Batty.

"Goddess, no!" he exclaimed in horror at the sight before him.

The poachers must have realized they were running out of time. Fires scorched the moon for as far as he could see. Dozens of poachers on skimmers drove the Tasiers into massive traps. What horrified him the most was that in the distance there was a machine drilling into the side of a mountain—his mountain—the home of the Kingdom of Glitter.

CHAPTER NINE

"Faster, Batty," Tamblin encouraged, leaning low over the bat's neck.

Arosa clung to his waist. Batty quivered with fear as the flames rose, creating a turbulent current of superheated air. Tamblin's eyes burned from the smoke. He leaned to the left when a poacher's skimmer came into view.

His fury intensified when he saw the man aim his flamethrower at the ground. He could see terrified Tasiers scurrying for safety while the man laughed. A feeling of help-lessness overcame him at his inability to stop the alien.

Goddess, if you can hear me, please help us, he silently pleaded.

As if the Goddess had heard his request, the flame glowing at the end of the flamethrower's wand sputtered and went out. It was a fleeting moment of salvation for the poor Tasiers still running for their lives.

With that prayer answered, Tamblin looked toward the mountain ahead. He choked back his cry of rage when the tip of the drill bit disappeared into the rock. It looked like it might have broken through to the main chamber. His worst fears were confirmed when hundreds of mounted bats and sand skimmers emerged.

"Arosa, can you fly?" he urgently demanded.

"Yes," she breathlessly replied.

"I will get you as close as I can. I need you to find Tia and Arielle. Please make sure they get to safety," he instructed.

"Tamblin," she began.

He covered her hand with his and squeezed it. "Please. My people will need somewhere to go. Your kingdom may be our only hope," he said before he released her hand and pulled on Batty's rein. "Go!"

He gritted his teeth to keep from calling out to her when she rose behind him. Pressing his heels into Batty's side, he urged the bat forward. He pulled the staff from the pouch on the saddle and twisted the end. It seemed like a feeble defense against such overwhelming odds, but the power crystal and the remaining guardians were the only weapons available.

Arosa floated in the air, watching with growing horror and sadness. The loud shout of triumph from the poacher on the drilling machine drew the attention of his cohorts in crime. She recognized him as the one called Macron. The bright flares from the Leviathan warriors did little more than cause Macron to swear in a loud voice.

"Harron, fire the nets! Fire the nets!" Macron shouted.

Harron fired a weapon that sent a net over the opening, preventing any more warriors from flying out of the gaping hole the drill had created. She flew forward when a warrior was knocked off of his skimmer.

She wrapped her arms around the falling rider. Slender arms clung to her in shock. Arosa landed on an outcropping of rock a safe distance from the battle.

"Thank you, Goddess," a soft voice shakily said.

"Tia! What are you doing here? What has happened?" she anxiously asked.

Tia reached up and removed her helmet. A trickle of blood ran from a cut on her temple. Arosa looked into Tia's haunted eyes.

"Our home—my people—our world…." Tia incoherently said, looking around her before she continued, "We need your help, Goddess. Please—for the sake of my people, my daughter, Jett… and Tamblin, I beg you to help us."

Arosa swallowed and followed Tia's gaze. Aikaterina always said they were only to observe. But, hadn't Aikaterina helped the Valdier and other species when she gave them symbiots and the abilities to shift and harness their surrounding energy? Hadn't Aminta given gifts to each of the rulers of the Seven Kingdoms to guide and protect them?

How could she stand by and watch the destruction of this world when she had the power to save it? What was the purpose of having such power, if not to use it for good? As the questions and doubts assailed her, she realized that she would give up everything to protect this world and the man that she had fallen in love with—for life and her existence held no meaning otherwise.

"I was dishonest with him. I should have told him who I was," she said.

"He will forgive you," Tia promised.

She looked at Tia. A strange dampness blurred her vision, and she could feel it coursing down her cheeks. She wiped it away with her fingers.

"Tears… I didn't know we could cry," she confessed, looking at the moisture.

"You'll help us?" Tia asked, reaching for her hand.

Arosa closed her fingers around Tia's slender green hand. Her gaze remained fixed on Tamblin. He was trying to slice through a net that had entrapped dozens of warriors while Batty distracted the poacher nearby.

"Yes, I will help. I promised Tamblin that I would make sure that you and your daughter were safe first," she replied.

Tia's startled protest ended on a growl of frustration when Arosa opened a portal that would take Tia safely back to her daughter. Arosa smiled faintly. Now that her promise to Tamblin had been kept, she would keep the one she had made to Tia—regardless of the consequences.

"ENOUGH! This world is under my protection," she commanded.

As her command spread, Arosa grew larger. The illusion of her persona as the Queen of the Wood Fairies faded. Creatures large and small trembled when they saw the power of her natural form. She raised her arms and sent a wave of energy so powerful that the moon trembled and the ships in orbit lost power.

"Forget about the Dragon Lords killing us, Macron. We've gone and angered the Goddesses," Harron whispered in a hoarse voice.

CHAPTER TEN

Tamblin lost his balance and fell sideways when the line he was cutting through gave way. He was about to start on the next cable when the sound of Arosa's voice swept through him as if she were standing next to him. He braced his hand against the ground and looked around.

A shockwave of disbelief passed through him when he saw her. He rose unsteadily to his feet as the image of her as the Queen of the Wood Fairies faded, and in her place was a powerful, larger-than-life Goddess. He dropped down to one knee and bowed his head when she looked in his direction.

"Tamblin," she softly called.

He looked up at her before bowing his head again, curling his fingers into fists as he tried to comprehend what was happening. A movement to his left drew his attention. The net that had pinned the struggling warriors to the ground dissolved.

The faint sound of awe and hushed reverence washed through him. All around him, the poachers' nets turned to ash. The huge aliens dropped to their knees and bowed their heads.

"Goddess, we… uh… we were just… uh…," Macron stuttered.

"I know what you were doing. You were being… horrible," she snapped.

Despite his own sense of intimidation at seeing Arosa in this form and realizing who and what she was, he couldn't help being both proud and amused. Unable to resist, he raised his head and watched Arosa as she glided across the ground to the drilling machine Macron was sitting on. With a snap of her fingers, it vanished and the large male hit the ground.

"If you or any of your kind *ever* come back to this moon, harm or capture another Tasier, or even *think* of harming the species that live here, I swear it will be more than your drilling machine that disintegrates—it will be your spaceship while you are on it or worse! They are *under my protection*! Do you understand?" she demanded.

"Yes, ma'am. I mean, yes, Goddess. We'll never touch another Tasier or come to this place or anywhere near here again," Macron hastily promised.

"I won't either, Goddess," Harron swore.

"You will return every single Tasier that you took off of this moon, and if you find any others, you are to give them to the Valdier who will bring them here," she instructed.

"All of them…," Macron complained before he clamped his lips together when Harron elbowed him.

"We'll return them all, Goddess," Harron promised.

"That's a lot of credits. I mean, if we could keep…," Macron grumbled.

Arosa appeared in front of Macron. Tamblin winced when the man was yanked up off the ground and suspended in midair in front of her. Even in the early morning light, he could see the sweat beading on the alien's brow.

"I don't have to make you disappear all at once. I could start with one piece at a time. So what is more important, credits or—" Arosa paused and ran her furious eyes down over Macron's body before stopping at his crotch.

Several men next to Tamblin winced and snickered under their breath. "I'd pay an alien's credit to have her do it," one warrior chuckled.

He bit back his own laugh when Macron dropped his hands and covered the spot she was eyeing. Even some of the poachers snickered with amusement. After several seconds, she sneered and with a flick her wrist, Macron disappeared.

"Who wishes to be next?" she demanded, glancing over the cowering group of men with a regal stance. "You have one hour to return all the Tasiers to this world. The Valdier will ensure that you miss none of them."

Tamblin and the others of his kind stood and watched with a combination of relief and awe as the poachers hastily departed back to their transports. A hush fell over the group closest to him when Arosa looked at him.

He was trying to think of what to say to her when the world around him changed and he was suddenly in the cave they'd left earlier. He swayed and lifted a hand to his head. A slender arm wrapped around his waist when his knees almost gave out.

"I'm sorry. I used a little too much power. I'm not used to carrying others," she said in an apologetic tone.

He shook his head and immediately regretted it. A low moan slipped from him, and he sat down heavily on the bed that appeared under him. He dropped his hand to the royal blue silk covers.

"This… is a little out of place, don't you think?" he asked with a wry smile.

"Is it? I supposed it is," she ruefully replied, sitting down beside him.

He breathed deeply to calm his wildly beating heart and looked around. Arosa had indeed taken them back to the cave. It was the same—except for the bed.

He brushed his hand against hers and she glanced at him shyly, covertly brushing her fingers against his. He turned her hand over and caressed her palm with his thumb. She had taken the shape of the Fairy Queen.

"Why didn't you tell me who you really were?" he asked in a quiet voice.

"I wanted to, but I was afraid," she confessed.

He quickly looked up at her face and frowned. "You—afraid? Did you see how those huge aliens reacted to you? You made one dissolve with a snap of your fingers," he said in an incredulous tone.

She gave him a crooked smile. "Disappear—I sent him back to his ship in space. I wouldn't actually hurt him. Well, I could, but I would rather not if possible. Several Valdier warships have arrived, and they are searching the ships. I thought it would be good for him to have to face them," she confessed.

Tamblin considered Arosa's contrite expression and shook his head. "Why were you afraid?" he asked.

"How was I supposed to tell the man I fell in love with that I'm considered a Goddess on many worlds? How do I tell him that I'm older than the moon he calls home and as old as the star system he lives in? What was I supposed to tell him —" she said before he cut her off by capturing her lips in a passionate kiss.

She parted her lips, and he deepened the kiss. He slid his arms around her and pulled her down until she was lying on top of him. She wrapped her hands around his neck, her mouth moving against his.

When she rolled her hips against him, he broke the kiss, breathing heavily. Her swollen lips beckoned him for more. She looked nothing like the Goddess and everything like the woman he had fallen in love with, yet, he could see power in her unguarded eyes—the reflection of the universe… and love.

"You tell him just the way you did. I love you for you, Arosa. I love that you are kind and loving—and can scare away the bad guys with the snap of your fingers. I love you for who you are—here," he said, lifting his hand and laying it over her heart. "I hope you can love me the same way. I am but a simple King of a very small but proud species living in a cave on an isolated moon in a vast universe."

"You're perfect, Tamblin," she replied, bowing her head and capturing his lips again.

EPILOGUE

Valdier Scientific Research Ship, Harmony:

Orbit: Minor Moon of Leviathan

Mandra Reykill absently listened to the list of items the Harmony's Science Officer, Bale, was relaying to him. His attention was focused on his mate, who was growling—literally—at some unfortunate soul. He stepped through the door into the cargo hold and stopped.

She beautiful when she angry, his dragon growled with delight.

Yes, she is, Mandra agreed with a sigh.

Cages, stacked from floor to ceiling in rows of twenty, filled the cargo hold. Frightened, squeaking Tasiers filled nearly half of the units. However, it wasn't the Tasiers that captured his full attention; it was the beautiful rose and gold dragon snarling at a group of four Qualin poachers who had their hands high in the air. Given the guns on the floor, they seemed to have made the right decision to surrender. Leave it to his mate to find the poachers' stash before the rest of his men did. Two of his guards standing on each side of Ariel bowed their heads in his direction.

"What have you found out so far, *mi elila?*" Mandra asked, walking over to her.

Ariel's dragon form shimmered and she shifted back into her two-legged form. "I found out that these pieces of trash violated the restrictions regarding this moon and poached a protected species," she replied with a glare at the men.

"Hel… p. Please, someone hel…p me!" a pitiful voice called from one of the cages.

Mandra frowned and scanned the cages. Inside one was a shivering Qualin with ice crystals hanging from his nose. His knees were pressed to his chin in the narrow confines of the metal box, and his clothing was stiff as if frozen.

"He looks like he just came out of the freezer!" Ariel exclaimed.

"Get him out," Mandra ordered with a wave of his hand to Bale and another Valdier warrior.

The two men climbed the cages to the one on top. It took them several minutes, and a cutting tool, to open the cage. When they did, they had to pull the half-frozen man out by his legs and carefully bring him down to the deck with the help of two of the Qualin crew.

"What is your name and explain what happened," Mandra demanded.

The man tried to lift his chin, but he couldn't, so he just looked up. "M-Ma… cron, my… Lord. The G-God…d-dess," Macron stuttered.

Surprise swept through Mandra before he began to chuckle. Ariel and Bale looked at him with a curious expression. He shook his head. He knew exactly how mischievous the Goddesses could be. The last time, they had shrunk him, his brothers, and his extended family while on a camping trip— all so the kids could go on an adventure to find the King of the Leprechauns!

"Yes, well, by order of the Valdier, this moon is a protected habitat. We allow no one to harvest, sell, or harm any of the Tasiers or other inhabitants," Mandra stated.

"You... you don't have... to worry about me... *ever* coming back, my Lord. That... the Goddess threatened... to dissolve my... anyone if we did," Macron said with a low groan as he slowly stretched out his legs.

"Put him with the others until I decide what to do with them," Mandra instructed to Bale.

"Yes, sir," Bale replied.

He wrapped his arm around Ariel and guided her to the exit. She worriedly looked over his shoulder. He chuckled and kissed her temple.

"We'll safely release all of them," he promised.

She kissed him and smiled. "I know. I'm just a worrywart about having a bunch of Tasier-loving dragons releasing them," she confessed.

He threw his head back and laughed, then lifted her off her feet. Several warriors grinned with amusement as they passed by.

"Trust me when I say there isn't a dragon on any ship who would harm one of your precious animals with you around.

Besides, after the last incident with those damn creatures, I think the little furballs have lost their appeal," he said.

Lucky me, he thought, thinking of all the trouble the furry creatures had caused.

Lucky us, his dragon purred, thinking how happy his mate would be when the tiny creatures were safely released.

Minor Moon of Leviathan

Arosa was lying in Tamblin's arms with her head on his shoulder when a familiar presence drew her attention to the entrance of the cave. She brushed her fingers tenderly along Tamblin's relaxed face. He was sleeping deeply—a combination of their lovemaking and his exhaustion from the last few months of conflict.

She faded, reforming next to the bed. A gown appeared around her, and she glided across the cave to the entrance. A smile brightened her face when she saw Arilla waving her arms like a conductor in front of an orchestra. Beyond, the burnt ground transformed as a light rain fell. Colorful mushrooms pushed up through the ground to carpet the once scorched landscape.

Thank you, sister, Arosa said as she floated over to her.

"You're welcome," Arilla replied with a grin.

"Where have you been?" she asked.

Arilla shrugged. "Exploring, checking in on old friends, giving my sister time to find out where her heart truly belongs," she stated.

"I didn't realize we could have a heart—until now," she replied.

Arilla smiled in response. They stood side-by-side, gazing out at the world. Arosa watched as dozens of transports arrived on the planet. A swift search of the vessels reassured her it was only the Valdier returning the confiscated Tasiers to the moon.

"What will happen next, Arilla? I love him. I can't imagine existing without him," she said.

"You'll be happy," Arilla responded, threading her arm through Arosa's.

"Aikaterina—" she began in a hushed tone.

Arilla laughed and squeezed her arm. "I don't think you need to worry about Aikaterina. She has her own challenges to deal with, thanks to us," she retorted in a reassuring tone.

Arosa looked at her sister. "What will you do?" she asked.

Arilla wiggled her nose. "I'll explore more worlds, visit my sister occasionally, help the Dragonlings get into mischief, and try to stay one step ahead of the Elders," she said.

"It sounds like you are on a mission," she reflected.

Arilla laughed. "Yes, I guess I am. What do you think?" she asked, waving a hand at her handiwork.

Arosa gazed out at the healed landscape and smiled. "Beautiful, just like you," she teased.

"I'll miss you, Arosa," Arilla confessed.

"I'll miss you, too, sister," she said.

She trailed her fingers along Arilla's arm as she slowly vanished. A smile of contentment curved her lips. She wondered if the universe was ready for a renegade Goddess on a mission. The thought caused her to laugh.

"What's so funny?" Tamblin asked, sliding his arms around her waist and pulling her back against him.

"I thought you would still be asleep," she teased.

He kissed her neck. "I missed you. You've been busy," he said.

"A gift from my sister Arilla," she confessed.

"Will you stay with me?" he quietly inquired.

She heard the note of uncertainty in his voice. She turned in his arms and caressed his cheek. He gazed at her with a look that laid bare his soul. The love shining in his eyes took her breath away and made her want to cry—in a good way.

"I love you, Tamblin. My heart belongs to you," she said, grasping his hand and pressing it against her chest.

"You will always be my Arosa. The beautiful Queen of the Wood Fairies who captured my heart," he murmured before capturing her lips in a passionate kiss.

Valdier:

Several months later

"So tells me what's the matters," Morah Reykill said, adjusting her golden glasses.

"I've met a man—a human—and I'm not sure what to do. One minute I want to feel his touch, and the next, I'm seriously considering burying him up to his neck in the ground," Arilla confessed, lying back against the pillows on Morah's bed.

Morah tapped on the tablet she was holding and looked over the rim of her glasses. "You's comes to the right person for advice," she calmly said.

Note from the Author:

I hope you enjoyed Tamblin and Arosa's story. The characters from the Kingdom of Glitter and Sandora captured my imagination when I first wrote about them in *Ambushing Ariel*. After writing *For the Love of Tia* and *The Dragonlings and the Magic Four-Leaf Clover*, I knew I would have to write Tamblin and Arosa's story. Yet, as you can imagine, I've also fallen in love with the mysterious, powerful, and charming 'Goddesses'. Arosa and Arilla captured my heart the moment they first appeared in my series. So, as much as this will probably get me in a lot of trouble, there will be more stories from the Dragon Lords, the Dragonlings, and yes—there will even be one for a **Renegade Goddess**.

PS: Don't forget to look for Easter Eggs to some of my other series!!

And if you're craving another PG-13 romantic adventure, one of my favorites is:

First Awakenings

Lieutenant Commander Ashton "Ash" Haze has gotten into some outrageous situations following his best friend, but this one really takes the cake. Ash is in a whole other galaxy now, separated from his team—who could have landed anywhere —and well, it's sure to be an adventure!

Kella Ta'Qui is a Turbinta, a member of a guild who discard their genetic identities in favor of what they train to become: assassins. Her first mission is to kill whatever was inside the unusual capsule that landed on Tesla Terra, but predator becomes prey when she is wounded by her target. She stumbles into a group who plan to sell her to the highest bidder— and her target rescues her.

Ash and Kella's alliance is like none this galaxy has ever seen! But will it lead to happy ending?

With endearing characters, daring escapes, nail-biting battles, and love found in the most unlikely of places, I hope you'll like this book as much as I do!

~Susan

ADDITIONAL STORIES

If you loved this story by me (S.E. Smith) please leave a review!

You can discover additional books at http://sesmithya.com. There you can also sign up for my newsletter to hear about my latest releases!

Find your favorite way to keep in touch below:

Newsletter direct link: http://eepurl.com/bBgI6v

RSS Feed: http://feeds.feedburner.com/MyFeedName

Facebook: https://facebook.com/YABooksSESmith

Twitter: https://twitter.com/SESmithYA

Pinterest: https://www.pinterest.com/SESmithYA/

Youtube: https://goo.gl/AjsvBt

Tumblr: http://sesmithya.tumblr.com/

Instagram: https://instagram.com/sesmithya/

Epic Science Fiction / Action Adventure

Project Gliese 581G Series

An international team leave Earth to investigate a mysterious object in our solar system that was clearly made by someone, someone who isn't from Earth. Discover new worlds and conflicts in a sci-fi adventure sure to become your favorite!

First Awakenings

Survivor Skills

New Adult / Young Adult

Breaking Free Series

Makayla steals her grandfather's sailboat and embarks on a journey that will challenge everything she has ever believed about herself.

Voyage of the Defiance

Capture of the Defiance

Makayla is older now, but when she needs help, her friends from years ago join new and unexpected allies. Capture of the Defiance is a thriller mystery that stands on its own as danger reveals itself in sudden, heart-stopping moments.

The Dust Series

Fragments of a comet hit Earth, and Dust wakes to discover the world as he knew it is gone. It isn't the only thing that has changed, though, so has Dust...

Dust: Before and After (Book 1)

Dust: A New World Order (Book 2)

Dragonlings of Valdier

The Valdier, Sarafin, and Curizan Lords had children who just cannot stop getting into trouble! There is nothing as cute or funny as magical, shapeshifting kids, and nothing as heartwarming as family.

The Dragonlings and the Magic Four-Leaf Clover

ABOUT THE AUTHOR

S.E. Smith is an ***internationally acclaimed***, ***New York Times and USA TODAY Bestselling*** author of science fiction, romance, fantasy, paranormal, and contemporary works for adults, young adults, and children. She enjoys writing a wide variety of genres that pull her readers into new worlds.

Printed in Great Britain
by Amazon

59652328R00061